THE
PRINCESS
COLLECTION

Princess Celestia and The Summer of Royal Waves

Written by G. M. Berrow

Little, Brown and Company
New York Boston

Little, Brown and Company

Hachette Book Group
1290 Avenue of the Americas, New York, NY 10104
Visit us at lb-kids.com

Little, Brown and Company is a division of
Hachette Book Group, Inc.
The Little, Brown name and logo are trademarks of
Hachette Book Group, Inc.

The publisher is not responsible for websites (or their content)
that are not owned by the publisher.

First Edition: April 2015

Library of Congress Control Number: 2014047878

ISBN 978-0-316-41086-1

10 9 8 7 6 5 4 3 2

RRD-C

Printed in the United States of America

For the two
most magical fillies I know—
Arabella and Beatrix

Contents

CHAPTER

1

Sunrise ♥ Over Canterlot

The sunlight dappled across the castle floor in multicolored shards, softening the appearance of the checkered stones with warmth and energy. The gentle haze of daybreak had always been Princess Celestia's favorite time. Not just because she was in charge of raising the sun. To her, the dawn was a peaceful and quiet promise of things to come—activities of the exciting day still lay ahead of all the ponies in the land. Today would be a beautiful sunrise.

Celestia turned to the sun and focused her magic. She watched the progression of the golden orb climbing higher into the sky, turning her attention back to the pattern projected onto the floor every so often with the focused care of an artist creating a grand masterpiece. Even though this picture was one that the princess had painted the same way each morning for hundreds of moons, she gave it the same care every single day. It was her honor and duty.

The pieces of stained glass set in the center of the main arched window depicted

Equestria's newest princess—an exceptionally talented young scholar named Princess Twilight Sparkle. The new royal and her five best pony friends and dragon assistant, whose images were immortalized in the glass as well, had protected Equestria from peril on more than one occasion. They now nobly sought to spread the true spirit of the Elements of Harmony and, in turn, the Magic of Friendship across its lands. Twilight Sparkle, Rainbow Dash, Rarity, Pinkie Pie, Applejack, Fluttershy, and Spike had come a long way since they'd all become friends. Celestia beamed with pride whenever the young heroes graced her thoughts or when their image in the window caught her attention.

A prominent piece of purple glass in the

window cast a glow in the shape of a star on the center tile of the floor, signaling that the morning process was almost complete. Celestia closed her almond-shaped eyes, and her dark lashes pressed down in stark contrast against her white cheekbones. She mustered every inch of strength in her body. She felt herself glistening with magical energy, from the bottom of her gilded hooves to the edges of her flowing mane of lavender, pale green, and periwinkle blue and bursting out to the very tip of her long, pearled horn. When Celestia opened her eyes again, the sun had reached the highest peak of its arc in the sky. The world was bright.

"*Gratias ad solis ortum,*" the princess recited as she bowed deeply to the sun.

"Thank you for allowing me to guide you, and thank you for another day of light."

"Beautifully done, sister."

"Thank you, Luna." Celestia smirked without turning around. "I did think that sunrise was particularly smooth."

"'Twas, indeed." Princess Luna stifled a yawn as she stepped forward to meet her elder sister. The contrast of the rich, velvety darkness of Luna's blue hide next to Celestia's pale, pearly complexion was stark. It mirrored the colors of the skies that they each watched over. Light and dark. Night and day.

But the sisters were not so different. In addition to raising the sun and the moon, they both ruled over Equestria, protecting its inhabitants from harm.

"You seem more exhausted than usual, Luna." Celestia furrowed her brow in concern as her sister yawned again. "Was the night not tranquil?"

"I must confess," Luna offered with a deep exhale, "I am feeling the effects of a nighttime most threatened." She pointed her hoof toward the eastern window of the throne room. "Peril on the coast."

"The coast? Tell me, sister," Celestia urged. "What happened? Is there anything I need to attend to on this day?" Celestia tried to remain calm as she spoke her words. Perhaps it was because she'd had hundreds of moons of experience dealing with crises under her crown, or perhaps she knew that panicking was the quickest way to derail a solution. Deep breaths and a steady voice were the key. Always maintain a calm composure, and those around would follow suit.

Princess Luna shook her head. Her dark, flowing mane billowed around the sides of her face. "It was just a manticore disturbance on the coastline," Luna explained, lifting her hoof toward the east. "Once my presence was known, I was able to reason with them. Until the Carcinus showed up... *He* came out of nowhere." She raised her brow in mild exasperation. Luna was tough, so this minor display signaled that the disaster was worse than it had been recounted.

Celestia stiffened. "Carcinus again?" she said with a frown, picturing the beast in her mind. The giant crab species were the size of small buildings and could be quite temperamental. But they were also gentle and understanding. A pony just had to know how to talk to them, to use kindness. "There have been far too many disturbances for my liking as of late. Perhaps I should not go to Monacolt after all. I'll just head to Horseshoe Bay and—"

"Sister, *no.*" Luna stepped in to block Celestia's path to the door. Her face grew stern. "You must keep your promise to Duchess Diamond Waves. You're the only pony who can help her, correct?"

"She seems to believe that the students at her magic school need my help." Celestia bit her lip and reconsidered. It was a struggle for her to relinquish responsibility of Equestria by leaving the capital, but even more of a struggle to let down an old friend in her hour of need. Celestia nodded. "You're right. I must go to her. With any luck, I'll have the students of Monacolt back on track within a few risings of the sun."

Celestia glided toward the balcony again, and Luna soon stood beside her. Both princesses watched over the stirrings of the waking city below in silent reverence. The Canterlot ponies were just beginning to fill the cobblestone paths.

A pair of royal guards in their golden armor trotted toward the castle, their blue-feathered helmet plumes bobbing up and down as they stepped in time. Across the main plaza, a milk pony was making his morning rounds and placing glass bottles of fresh cream in front of each café and residence. On the other side, a group of rambunctious colts and fillies trotted together, giggling and teasing one another. Celestia smiled to herself as she watched them surreptitiously. Her young unicorn students were vivacious—bright as the sun and bursting with talent. What could be so different about the students at Diamond Waves's academy? Celestia wondered. Whatever the reason for their struggle, Princess Celestia was about to find out. She'd be lying if she said she wasn't intrigued by the adventure.

CHAPTER

2

The Princesses of Equestria

Princess Luna raised an eyebrow at Celestia. "Are you really asking me that again?" The blue mare trotted around her sister in a circle, wondering if her sibling would ever learn to trust her. Celestia hardly ever let anypony know when she was worried, but Luna always could tell. And right now, Celestia's golden neckplate jewelry was on slightly crooked. Otherwise, Celestia was the picture of perfection.

"I know I need to start my journey, for it is long, but I just want to be absolutely sure," Celestia replied from the seat of the carriage. A soft pink glow came from her horn. She lifted a saddlebag bearing a picture of her golden sun cutie mark onto the seat next to her. "You're positive you can handle Canterlot on your own? Even with the situation at Horseshoe Bay?"

"I wish you would have more faith in me, Celie."

"I do, it's just that—"

Luna's face grew serious. "All right, you caught me. I'm planning to transform to Nightmare Moon mode as soon as you leave the border!" It was her favorite way to fuss with Celestia. After Luna had acted up and been banished to the moon, her sister was very touchy about the subject. But the two sisters were past that now. Celestia rolled her eyes, and Luna's face broke into a devious smirk. "Just teasing you, sister. I know that you worry about me watching over the day, so I've brought in somepony who is very competent to help out at your school and to look over Canterlot while I rest."

"Surprise!" a purple Alicorn with a pink star-shaped cutie mark trotted up to meet them. "Princess Luna said you needed a little bit of assistance."

"Twilight Sparkle!" Celestia exclaimed, embracing the pony. "What a pleasure it is to see you again, my faithful student. I hope you're not too put out by this request."

"Not at all, Princess," Twilight replied with a grin. "I can think of nothing more exhilarating than watching over your class for a few days." Twilight revealed a gigantic jalopy full of books. "In fact, I've even brought some special reading material that I know your students will be delighted with! I can't wait to discuss Wing Theory with them. Have you guys covered metamorphosis spells yet? Maybe I'll start with the good old apple-to-orange experiment." Twilight laughed and added, "I'll make sure all the class frogs are out of the room for that one." She winked. Twilight had once accidentally transformed a poor frog into an orange by mistake.

"Thank you," Celestia smirked. "Whatever lessons you decide to work on, I know my colts and fillies are in good hooves now. But, Twilight?"

"Yes, Princess?" Twilight perked up,

eyes wide and purple wings outspread. She looked electric with excitement about her impending stint in academia.

"Please make sure they have a little *fun* as well, okay? It's almost the summer break, for Star Swirl's sake." Celestia nudged the young Alicorn with her hoof. "You have a good time, too."

Luna giggled. Twilight crinkled her eyes in confusion. "What's not fun about speed-reading through the entire *Encyclopedia Equestria* and then quizzing each other on it?"

Celestia laughed, patting her faithful student on her purple mane. "You be sure to let me know when you figure it out, Twilight."

"Oooh! With a letter update?" Twilight Sparkle brightened. "Just like I used to?"

Celestia's thoughts flashed to the mountain of letters about friendship from Twilight in that one closet of her bedroom quarters. "On second thought, only send me a letter *if necessary*—to update me on the kingdom news. You and Princess Luna together, okay?" That seemed to be a good compromise and a perfect way to set Celestia's mind at ease.

"That's it?" Twilight's face contorted. "But what if I learn about—"

"We'll do just as you ask, sister," Luna interrupted, bowing her head. She winked at her sister. Twilight was obviously still learning to rein it in. "No more. No less. We promise you that. Right, Princess Twilight?"

"Of course." Twilight sighed, fighting her addiction to friendship letters. The princesses smiled and waved their hooves at Celestia. "Have a wonderful trip!"

"I shall try." Celestia nodded solemnly. She thought of her friend's desperate plea and couldn't help but imagine it wasn't going to be much of a lighthearted vacation. Celestia trotted off down the corridor to pack her saddlebags, reassuring herself with the fact that the kingdom would be just fine in her absence. She only looked back over her shoulder at Twilight and Luna twice to make sure that nothing had gone awry yet.

CHAPTER

3

A Princess Abroad

Afew hours and a thousand miles later, Princess Celestia was beginning to feel a twinge of anticipation about the impromptu visit, despite the worried tone of her friend's letter. Teaching another group of Unicorn students wasn't going to be difficult. Compared to what Celestia had to contend with in the past few moons, it would be downright simple. Celestia dealt with threatening foes in addition to running her own magical academy. At least the return of Princess Luna from the moon and the rise of Twilight Sparkle and her friends had eased some of the pressure of events such as Discord's attempt to seize the kingdom, a full-fledged changeling attack, and the near rescue of the Crystal Empire from evil King Sombra's curse. This was probably all just an elaborate ploy by Duchess Diamond Waves to get her friend to visit. Yes, Celestia decided, she had plenty of relaxation and catching up over tea awaiting her in the far-away land.

"We're almost there!" Princess Celestia shouted ahead to her royal guard companions. They flapped their wings and bore to the right to ready for descent.

Princess Celestia took a satisfying breath and peered down onto the landscape below. For the past hour, they'd been flying over green countryside filled with rolling hills, punctuated by quaint little villages. But the true jewel of the territories surrounding Prance was the coastal state of Monacolt. And it was growing nearer with each passing minute. Celestia inhaled the familiar sweet scent of pastries from the decadent bakeries mixed with fresh salt air of the ocean and felt happy.

When it came into view, Celestia gasped in reverence. Monacolt was the epitome of glamour, recognizable by its lavish structures trimmed in gold details and docks filled with hundreds of boats of all sizes. Celestia always loved how they swayed in the water, their tall masts waving as if they were saying hello just to her. As the carriage began its descent through the clouds, Celestia began to rack her brain for why she hadn't visited Duchess Diamond Waves sooner. She loved this gorgeous city by the sea. Last time Celestia had visited, she remembered standing on the beach at the little inlet known as Unicorn Cove, watching the waves crash up against the sandy cliffs. The blue droplets glittered in her warm sun, splashing upon her muzzle and mane. The water looked calmer today.

"Would you like us to land on the beach again, Highness?" one of the Pegasus royal guards called back to her. His blue mane rustled in the wind, hitting the sides of his golden helmet.

"Just in front of the school, please," Princess Celestia directed her guards as she brought her attention back to the reason she'd traveled to Monacolt in the first place. "I'm already late. Lessons ought to have begun for the day, and the duchess will be expecting me. She gets very upset when things don't run on schedule." Celestia watched Unicorn Cove disappear behind them, and a sad feeling hung low in the bottom of her stomach. "Maybe tomorrow I'll stop by," she added as a promise to herself.

"As you wish." The Royal Guard ponies soared through the city and finally touched their hooves down onto the ground. Though normally stoic, the stallions couldn't help but suppress a smirk at their beautiful surroundings. Glimmering Shield, the lead pony, nudged his partner Golden Flight, pointing his hoof at a row of brightly lit buildings across the plaza. The oscillating blue and orange lightbulbs promised CARD GAMES & CIDER as well as APPLE TREATS & AMAZING FEATS. The guards always argued over which ponies got to accompany Celestia on trips abroad. Monacolt was, in particular, a destination they all wished to visit. These two had hit the jackpot of assignments, and they knew it.

"Gentlecolts?" Celestia raised her brow at the two mesmerized stallions.

"Oh! Apologies, Highness!" The guards snapped to attention and cleared their throats, bowing low to their princess. "Please welcome her Grand Royal Highness to your beautiful land—preeeeesenting the princess Celestia of Canterlot! Protector of the sacred sun and all that its golden light touches for all of time and—"

"That's quite enough, Glimmering Shield." Celestia laughed. As the carriage steps unfurled onto the glittering cobblestone street, Celestia grew anxious to disembark and stretch her wings. She had placed but one hoof on the ground before she heard a familiar voice.

"Celie!" Duchess Diamond Waves, a tall, willowy Unicorn mare trotting out the main door of the school building, exclaimed with an inviting smile upon her sweet lemon-colored face. Instead of a crown, she wore a golden band across her forehead. "Do my eyes deceive me? Is it really you? Or is it some changeling sent to trick me?!"

Princess Celestia made a love-sucking vampire face just like Queen Chrysalis, using her magic to grow some fake fangs for added effect. The duchess gasped in mock horror. The two ponies laughed and embraced. It was like they had never been apart. True friends always picked up right where they left off. Princess Celestia put her hoof on Diamond Waves's back. "It feels like it's been a hundred moons!"

"Only fourteen, but who's counting?" the duchess teased. "Actually, I was."

"Far too long." Princess Celestia shook her head. "But I'm here now, and I'm so glad to see you, my dear friend."

"And I, you. But..." Diamond's face fell, and her voice began to quaver. "But it means so much more since...since I have nopony else in the world to turn to right now." Duchess Diamond Waves looked to the ground, and her ocean of blue mane locks fell down in a cascading waterfall to the stones. They weren't as shiny as Celestia remembered, and her tail wasn't fashioned into its usual perfect waves of varying light blues. And was her cutie mark of a glittering blue seashell looking dull as well? Diamond Waves didn't look like herself. She looked tired.

"Are you all right, Diamond?" Celestia asked in the gentlest tone. "You seem so... different."

"So you noticed that my mane isn't sparkling?" The duchess smoothed her mane and sighed heavily, the weight of stress visible on the Unicorn's delicate shoulders. "It hasn't for a while, actually. But let's not talk about manes; let's get to business—my school."

Celestia frowned in concern. "What is the matter?"

The duchess shook her head robotically, getting lost in her thoughts. "*None* of my students are ready for what lies ahead...."

"I'm surprised you even have them here in the summer!" Celestia teased. "My students are just finishing up back in Canterlot." She looked around at the beautiful weather and realized all it was missing was a bunch of young ponies reveling in it. They should have been down by the beach, splashing in the surf and collecting shells. Playing hide-and-seek in the ocean caves. Anything but studying.

"I had no choice. They had to be kept here because they didn't pass their exams. It's the first moon in Monacolt's history that it has ever occurred," Diamond Waves whimpered. "My father would have been so ashamed of me if he were still here. That's why I need you, Celie."

"Don't despair, Di." Celestia looked Diamond straight in her cool blue eyes and smiled. "Whatever is going on here at your academy, it doesn't stand a chance against you and me together. Just as nothing did before." Celestia lowered her horn and expelled a soft glow of blue sparkling magic toward the duchess. It enveloped the yellow pony and lifted her spirits enough to smile back at her friend a hint of newfound confidence. And it would have lasted longer, if it weren't for the bloodcurdling scream that came from inside the school two seconds later.

CHAPTER

4

Well-Behaved unicorns

Celestia and Diamond Waves crossed under the gilded archway sign that read MONACOLT MAGIC ACADEMY, tore through the doors, and galloped inside the school's main atrium. Celestia braced herself for attack, mustering her remaining strength from the day's journey to defend this land from mortal peril. She just couldn't believe it was happening before she'd even had the chance to sit down and have some Monacoltian apple crisp!

"Halt!" Celestia shouted into the void. Her beautiful mane and tail billowed out behind her as she searched the cavernous main entry for a menacing beast. "Let it be known that any creature that threatens any citizen of Monacolt must answer to me—Princess Celestia!" she bellowed. Celestia almost didn't recognize her own words, which sounded more like the tone of Princess Luna's when she had become Nightmare Moon than the gentle melody of her own voice. But a young pony was in danger. Where was the poor student that had signaled the alarm with their innocent scream? Hopefully they were unharmed and concealed somewhere, awaiting rescue. Celestia scanned the room. The duchess had disappeared.

"Eeeeeeeeek!" Another scream rang out, echoing down the empty school hallway. Celestia spun around, but there was nothing there. Could Discord have followed Celestia here to play a prank on her? She recalled a time when the naughty draconequus had covered himself in something called Invisipaint and followed her for an entire week, whispering everything she said right after she'd said it just to amuse himself. At the time, Celestia had thought she was going crazy. Right now, she thought it unlikely that this was any sort of trick.

The screaming suddenly stopped, followed by the sound of hooves and the muffled voice of Diamond Waves. "Now, what did you learn from this?" she hissed. Celestia followed the sounds to find that there was no monster at all, just a tiny blue Unicorn standing next to her friend, looking upset.

"I'm sorry, I just needed a snack. My tummy was grumbling and I couldn't think, and I—" The colt shifted back and forth on his hooves as he looked up at the headmistress. His eyes darted up to the mare and back down to the floor. "I, uh, learned to never leave class with-with-without a pass. Or you get attacked by a fake spider spell."

Diamond Waves leaned down toward the colt. "Repeat it again, just how I taught you, Rainy Air," the duchess said, jaw clenched.

"Y-y-yes, Headmistress Waves." Rainy Air nodded that he understood. "I shall not leave class without a pass, for the pony who leaves class does not pass."

"Good colt," Diamond Waves said, standing tall once more. She gave him a tiny smile. "I need focus from all of you. Only serious and talented Unicorns are allowed to stay at my academy. It is an honor and a privilege to be here. You understand, right?"

"Yes, Headmistress," Rainy Air replied. He crinkled his muzzle. "It's just that we finished reading the textbook assignment on fighting manticores that you told us to, and I thought I had time to—"

"Read the next section, then," Diamond Waves shot back. "Tell the others to do the same. I'm busy showing our guest teacher, Princess Celestia, around, and I need all of you to be ready to attempt your attack spells when we get to class."

"Yes, Headmistress," Rainy Air nodded. "I will do that and—"

"Hello there, little one," Princess Celestia called as stepped out of the shadows. She nodded her head in greeting to the duo.

"Celestia!" Duchess Diamond Waves brightened like a switch had been flipped. She chuckled. "It was nothing to worry about. Rainy Air here just got a little spooked."

"Rainy Air, is it?" Celestia smiled at the young pony and bent down. "You seem like you could use a snack." A glow of magic swirled from her horn and spun around, creating a beautiful red apple. Celestia passed it over to the colt, whose eyes were alight with wonder. The surface of the apple was so shiny, his reflection danced on its surface. The princess bowed to the student. "Nice to meet you. I'm Princess Celestia of Canterlot."

"Whoa," Rainy Air marveled. "That was so cool! Thank you." He crunched down on the crispy fruit and smiled back. "Now, there's a spell we should learn, Headmistress Waves!" he hollered before trotting back down the hallway and through the open classroom door.

"These colts and fillies." Duchess Diamond Waves shook her head in defeat. She trotted over to an arched window and looked out to the street. "See? They just don't understand how to take anything seriously. At this rate, none of them are going to pass their exams."

"It's true that exams are very important,

but you mustn't worry so much," offered Princess Celestia. "In the pursuit of education, all lessons can be learned if only you allow enough time for them. *Patience.*"

"I wish I could be patient…but I can't. Maybe you'll understand when you see this." The duchess motioned for Celestia to follow, and the two ponies headed to the heart of the school. They trotted through the halls, hooves clicking lightly on the marbled floor until they reached the Mane Hall. Celestia noticed that the wooden walls of the school were decorated with grandiose banners of the royal cutie marks of Monacolt in a rainbow of colors. They reached high up to the arched beams of the roof, a constant reminder to the Unicorn students of the history that had brought them there. A coin, a starfish, a crown, a rain cloud, a sand castle, and a seashell.

Celestia bowed to the banners in respect. They had been her great allies throughout the history of Equestria. "In the name of Unicorn, Pegasus, and Earth pony—I offer my regards."

"Celie, look!" Diamond Waves interrupted, motioning to a massive hourglass. "Time is the only thing we do not have." The hourglass was forged from silver, mounted on a marbled pillar and filled with golden sand. The grains funneled down into the bottom glass chamber in swirls and wispy loops. It was no ordinary timekeeper.

"The Time Glass?" Celestia gasped. She touched her hoof to the hourglass. "I didn't know it was here." The Alicorn marveled at the way her glorious sunlight shone down onto it through the skylight in the ceiling. "The last time I heard of it was over five hundred moons ago. I thought it had been destroyed."

Duchess Diamond Waves sighed. "Luckily, no."

Celestia watched the sand fall through the glass, mesmerized by its beauty. "King Nautilus must have been quite proud of you for continuing his tradition of educational excellence to let you keep the Time Glass here."

"Yes." Duchess Diamond Waves nodded. "In fact, it was the whole reason my father wanted me to open the school—I just know it. That's why it's such a crisis that"—Duchess Diamond Waves stifled a

sniffle—"the training of these young unicorns has been a failure. I don't want to fail
him and put Monacolt in danger!"

"How are you putting Monacolt in danger?" Celestia looked up at the hourglass
again, searching. But she saw nothing of a
threatening energy surrounding the Time
Glass. Just a gorgeous sculpture made of
metal and glass and carved with images
of Monacolt's history. There were pictures
of stars scattered onto the sandy shoreline, waves crashing against the cliffs, and
ponies of the region standing together in
reverence of it all.

"The sands of time are about to run
out," Diamond Waves said as she pointed
to the swirling sand. She leaned in close
to Celestia, eyes wide with terror, lowering

her voice to a whisper. "When they do, it is said that the ponies of Monacolt will have to protect the borders from a great invasion of beasts."

Celestia frowned. "In all my moons, I have not heard this legend. I understood the Time Glass to be nothing more than a magical object that kept the days of the calendar. Why did you never speak of this threat, Duchess?"

Diamond Waves began to pace back and forth, her nerves trying to escape through her hooves. "I thought that we had at least another Circle of the Comets before the event...that's what the ponies in Northern Prance say. But I was wrong. I thought we had more time to impress upon these youths that they *need* to train. Because it can only be daughters and sons of this land that can fulfill this destiny to protect us." Diamond Waves gestured to the Mane Hall, lined with classroom doors. "Thank goodness you are here to fix everything, Celestia. You're my only hope."

Celestia looked up to the hourglass once more and back to the panicked expression on her friend's face. "I'll do what I can."

"Thank you for understanding. I need every student to pass the beast defense spells exams on the next try. If not, I've…I've failed." Diamond's face grew stern. "As an educator and as a protector of Monacolt."

Celestia and Diamond looked up toward the last banner in the sequence. It was the same color as Diamond Waves's beautiful mane, and the emblem of a seashell stitched onto it was the mark that graced the duchess's very own flank. She was destined and determined to protect this land, no matter what. So would Celestia.

CHAPTER

5

Lesson Number Fun

The next morning, Princess Celestia felt rather awkward as she stood at the head of the classroom. She wasn't sure why the students looked so afraid of her, but there they were—twelve Unicorns staring back at her with expressions of pure terror. Nopony was talking or giggling as her students back in Canterlot did before class began each day. When Duchess Diamond Waves had briefed Celestia the previous evening before she'd left for her impromptu visit to the ponies up north, she'd reiterated that her students were lacking focus. It seemed like a false assessment, so Celestia wasn't sure what to believe from the stack of notes her friend had provided. It was time to experiment.

"Good morning, fillies and colts!" Celestia chirped, hoping to stir a reaction with her sunny smile. Nopony even blinked an eye. They were like the stone statues in the Canterlot garden.

"My name is Princess Celestia," she continued on. She used her magic to write her name on the board with a piece of chalk. "I'm an old friend of Headmistress Diamond Waves, and I'm here to help you with some of your spells while she's away in Northern Prance. Let's start with something simple, shall we?" Celestia began to pace back and forth, but then thought better of it. She didn't want to spook any of these little ponies. She stopped and sat down, trying to match their stillness. She took off her gold crown and put it on the desk to show the students they could see her as an equal. "Does anypony know what a Windigo is?"

A magenta curly-maned Unicorn filly in the front row raised her hoof. Celestia looked at the seating chart. "Hello, my dear. Are you Ambrosia Breeze, perchance?"

"Yes, Princess." Ambrosia Breeze nodded, keeping her eyes cast down at her desk. She began to speak robotically. "A-Windigo-

is-an-evil-spirit-that-feeds-off-fighting-and-
hatred-but-can-be-defeated-by-any-'love
fire'-such-as-friendship-fire-or-caring-fire."

"Excellent! That's exactly right." Celestia
laughed, and her almond eyes crinkled in
satisfied delight. "You're as clever as Clover
the Clever himself!" Ambrosia blinked her
green doe eyes in disbelief and looked to
her other classmates, who seemed just as
surprised by Celestia's response as she. The
princess, however, did not notice the rest of
the class's astonishment.

"Now..." Celestia continued, assuming
her natural teacher role. It was one she
felt completely comfortable in, despite not
being back home at her own school or guid-
ing her faithful student Twilight Sparkle.
"Does anypony know what other creatures
can be tamed with the Fire of Friend-

ship?" Five ponies immediately raised their hooves high into the air. "Wow!" Celestia exclaimed, scanning the hooves. "You tell us...Mr. Sandy Shore?"

"Manticores and hydras," answered the tan colt with the white mane, daring to smile a little bit. "Mainly," he added, just in case he was wrong. "There are probably others, too."

"Well done!" Celestia grinned. She looked around the room and nodded. "I have to say, you all are much more prepared than your headmistress thinks. I was expecting to have to start from scratch, but you all sure have done your homework." She trotted down the aisle of desks and noticed that each student had a thick scroll covered in writing on top of their tall stacks of books. She used her magic to pick up the one on Rainy Air's desk. "What's this, Rainy Air?"

"They're our essays, Miss Princess," a pale lavender filly with a straight teal mane squeaked. She stifled a yawn. "On defense spells. We do them every night to practice for the big Muybridge test."

"Muybridge?" Celestia repeated to herself. She'd never heard of it before. At her school, the only exam was simply called the Unicorn Final.

The lavender filly motioned for Celestia to lean in closer and said quietly, "Muybridge was an old stallion who won a battle in Monacolt a long time ago. Headmistress is obsessed with him, so we're always studying what he did and writing about how he fought the monsters. Our big exam is based on all the feats he accomplished."

"Flora! Shhh!" urged a yellow colt with a spiky green mane. "You'll get us in trouble. We're not supposed to tell anypony about that! It's top secret academy business."

"It's fine, Lemon Square. She's our new teacher, right? She's gonna know eventually...." said Rainy Air. He looked back at Celestia dreamily, admiring how her mane and tail floated continuously, sparkling in the daylight. He wondered how it did that and considered asking her, but thought better of it.

Ambrosia Breeze held up her scrolls, covered in writing. "We've had to write an essay every night this moon since Headmistress Diamond Waves got all strict and boring and horrible—" She covered her mouth. "Whoops. Please don't tell her I said that!" Lemon Square shot Ambrosia a knowing look and then rolled his eyes. Ambrosia frowned and slumped down.

But she wasn't the only pony who seemed grumpy and tired. All around the classroom, the students had their heads down on the desks, fighting to stay awake from their long night of homework. Celestia recalled that when her friend was younger, Diamond Waves had a tendency to get carried away with completing her assignments, like a certain young purple Alicorn back home. But there was a perfect cure for that.

Princess Celestia winked at Ambrosia. "Don't worry, class. Go ahead and take a rest if you need to. Just let me know. You can tell me anything. Everything that happens in this classroom is just between *us* students."

"But you're not a student...." Flora whispered timidly, looking around at her class-mates. "You're a…a…princess."

"Of course I'm a student!" Celestia replied. "A pony never stops learning, no matter how old they are or if they are royalty. For example, I just learned something from all of you."

"You did?" asked Rainy Air, leaning forward in curiosity. "Cool! I mean…what was it?"

"That you students are in desperate need of possessing the greatest power of all"—Celestia leaned forward and met their eyes—"the power of *fun*!" The word caused all the students to gasp in horror. They clearly had a long way to go.

CHAPTER

6

The Key to Magic

Celestia chuckled and used her magic to erase the chalkboard, which was filled with diagrams of great beasts, maps of Monacolt, and tactical spells. In its place, she drew a bunch of balloons that would have made Pinkie Pie proud. Then she drew some smiley faces. It was a start, at least.

"Fun?" the students whispered to one

another. "But this is school time! The head-mistress would be so mad if we had *fun*."

"Who can tell me about some things that are fun to do?" Celestia queried, ignoring the protests and continuing to use her magic to do away with everything that looked serious or boring. *Swish.* A bunch of posters on proper Unicorn spell-casting posture flew out the window. *Swoosh.* A banner that said STUDYING IS THE KEY TO MAGIC folded into a bouquet of paper flowers and landed on the teacher's desk.

"Oooh! I know!" Sandy Shore raised his hoof. "It's fun when I finish my essay for the night and my mom says I get to brush my teeth before bedtime!"

"Yeah!" agreed a pink filly with a straight mane. "I love that. All those minty bubbles dancing in my mouth are cool."

"Hmmm…" Celestia cocked her head to the side. "I suppose taking care of yourself is satisfying, yes. But what else makes you happy?"

"I like raindrops on roses," Rainy Air said with a casual shrug. "But that's more a *favorite* thing than a fun thing."

"Getting a little better," Celestia encouraged. "But think bigger. How about… galloping on the beach with the wind in your mane or singing songs with your friends around a campfire?"

The class considered this. A few young Unicorns looked as if they were straining to remember what a "campfire" was. Or maybe they actually didn't know what a campfire was.

"I like the sound of those activities in theory.…" Flora squeaked. Her already-big eyes began to widen even more. "But what if you're doing one of them and then you get in trouble for not doing your homework instead?" The students all nodded in agreement. This was much worse than Celestia thought. She needed something to truly light a fire in the hearts of these students to get them to loosen up. There had to be another strategy, a way to speak these students' language.

"Everypony, I'd like you to pair up into partners with your essays. You're going to practice a friendship fire spell."

"We are?" The ponies erupted into a flurry of whispers. "That's a hard one! Nopony's ever done it!"

"I'll give it a shot." Ambrosia Breeze trotted over and sat down next to Flora, using her magic to pass her essay over. Sandy

Shore and Rainy Air paired up as well. Soon the whole class had found partners. They looked up to Celestia, eagerly awaiting their next instructions.

"Oooh! Are we going to read each other's work and critique it first?!" Ambrosia Breeze shouted. "Because we've done this many times before and we're very good at it, just so you know." Ambrosia grinned and added, "By the way, this whole thing where we can talk without raising our hooves is awesome. So freeing." Ambrosia put her hoof to her mouth. "Don't tell the headmistress I said that."

"No, Ambrosia. We're not going to *read* the essays. We're going to do something a little different this time." Celestia walked over to Ambrosia and Flora and bent down to meet their faces. "I want you two to tear up each other's work." Somepony in the back of the room dropped a textbook. Princess Celestia giggled at their shocked faces.

"What?!" the two ponies shrieked in disbelief. "But we'll get in so much trouble!" Across the room, Sandy and Rainy were paralyzed with shock as well. Rainy held his essay close to his chest protectively. "And we worked so hard!"

"Sounds risky..." Celestia nodded with a sly look. "But kind of interesting, right?" A moment passed where nopony knew what the correct answer was at all. Was this a trick? Or a test that had been set up by Duchess Diamond Waves to see if they would succumb to such a temptation?

"It does!" Flora finally said, much louder than anything else she'd ever uttered in her life. Her voice didn't even squeak. It caused everypony to jump a little, and Ambrosia Breeze shot her partner an offended look. "I mean, it sounds kinda different and scientific…uh…for learning purposes and…oh, never mind," Flora whispered, retreating back into herself.

"Well, I'll give it a try. I'm not afraid of *anything*." Ambrosia Breeze snatched Flora's essay and used her magic to shred it to tiny pieces. *Rip, rip, rip.* They floated down to the ground pitifully, landing in a sad pile on the ground. Flora's jaw dropped. She lunged over and tore Ambrosia's scroll out of the air with her hoof. Flora showed no mercy, doing the exact same thing until both essays lay in one heap in between them. The whole class went silent.

"All that work, gone…" said Ambrosia

Breeze, breaking the silence. She looked down in horror at the pile of paper. "So much research lost…" Flora whispered, her lavender face the picture of true horror. Everypony leaned in, not wanting to make the even the slightest move. A few moments later, Flora started to giggle. Ambrosia couldn't help but join in. Then the giggling quickly evolved into full-blown laughter. Soon the whole class was laughing and tearing up one another's scrolls. It was a confetti explosion of essays.

And one by one, as the papers were destroyed, small blue-hued flames began to rise from the ruins. Celestia smiled to the class. "See, students? You did it! The Fire of Friendship defense burns!"

"But how did we finally complete the spell?" Rainy Air asked, gaping at the little blue heart-shaped flames rising from the remains of his homework. "We've been trying to do this one for ages."

"That's because it can only come from the bravery of two ponies offering friendship to each other despite a personal sacrifice," Celestia explained. "You all banded together even though you had something to lose." Slowly, smiles began to show up on the students' faces, and the classroom began to warm up as if it were a new dawn. And it wasn't from all the flames.

CHAPTER

7

Out of the Bubble

Stay with me, students." Princess Celestia turned back to the single-file line of Unicorns following her down the wooden steps. They whispered to one another excitedly, pointing toward the ocean shore. As they made their way to the beach, Celestia could feel their curiosity mounting with each hoofstep. Ambrosia Breeze skipped up to the front. "Princess, where are we going? What are we doing?" Her green eyes were wide with anticipation. She craned her neck, scanning the area, and whispered. "Is it school-related?"

"Oh yes. It's a surprise lesson, Ambrosia," Princess Celestia said with a wink. By now, she was used to the constant nervous questioning from the students. They always wanted to know what value they were going to get out of each class. It was like teaching a big group of Twilight Sparkles all at once. "It's going to be quite amusing and informative, I assure you." Celestia's long mane whipped in the ocean breeze. Her cheeks were a rosy pink in the golden sunlight.

"Okay!" Ambrosia bounced back to

Flora, and the two little ponies exchanged a look, then squealed. The rest of the class followed the pair, clopping their hooves against the wooden staircase that led down to the sand. Up on the street level of the Monacolt promenade, ponies started to spill out of the hotels and cafés to gather and watch. They whispered and pointed to the foreign royal, wondering what sort of show they might catch a glimpse of. They hadn't seen the students of the Monacolt Magic Academy out on a field trip in a very long time.

"All right, class," Princess Celestia announced, pacing around the group. Her hoofcuffs sunk down into the warm, dry sand. "Your assignment for today is to run, play, and jump. Look at the tide pools.

Study the clouds above. Take in everything, and then we'll all share with one another at the end of the day. Got it?" Celestia looked at their blank faces. "Basically, just have fun in the sun."

"Uhh." Lemon Square raised his hoof. "Princess?"

"Yes, Lemon Square?" Celestia trotted over to the yellow colt. "You have a question?"

"Is it true?" Lemon Square pointed to the sun, burning bright and high in the sky, squinting as if he hadn't seen it in a very long while.

"Is what true?"

"The sun! That you have the power to raise the sun? I did some research and—"

"Yeah, of course she can! She's an

Alicorn, Lemon," Ambrosia cut in, and rolled her eyes. "Everypony knows Alicorns are the most powerful ponies, like ever. *Ever.* They're super-duper rare, and you can only become one if you perform some amazing magical feat. There haven't been many except Mi Amore Cadenza, Twilight Sparkle, and—"

"So can we become Alicorns if we study harder?" shouted Sandy Shore from the back of the group. "Will you please make us Alicorns?!"

"I don't think I'd want to be an Alicorn," Flora said in her tiny voice. "Seems like too much, you know?" Sandy Shore nodded.

"I have an even better question." Rainy Air looked at Celestia with a dreamy expression. "How exactly do your mane and tail move like that all the time? It's really...uh, pretty."

"Yeah, it is." Ambrosia tilted her head to the side so she could admire Celestia's mane from another angle. "I think Headmistress Diamond Waves's mane used to do that."

"All right, students," Celestia said, hushing them. "There will be time for questions about me later. For now, just do as I say. You're out of a classroom, and you're standing on a beautiful beach! Make the most of it. I think you'll find it's worth your time to get out of your little schoolroom *bubble*." She gave a little smile and dispersed. A few looked back over their shoulders at the princess, just to make sure it was really okay. They were slowly but surely getting used to trusting her and letting go of their uptight demeanors. Celestia knew that Diamond

Waves was going to be pleased with the result.

"Bubble?" repeated Ambrosia Breeze to herself as she looked out at the vast body of water. She galloped off to join a game of hide-and-seek.

Up above by the cliff railing, the crowd of ponies watching grew thinner as the students ran off into little groups across the beach. It wasn't the magic show they were all hoping for. The colts and fillies really did just appear to be playing around, throwing sand at one another and diving into the water. A few older mares and stallions hung around, amused by the sight.

"Isn't it lovely, sweetie?" said an old gray stallion to his wife. They stood under a shady white umbrella. "The students have been let out of school."

"Oh yes," agreed the blue mare. She peered down through her circular glasses. "It's nice to finally see them enjoy the summer. It really livens the place up. We need it, especially since there aren't even waves on the water these days."

"Too quiet around here." The gray stallion nodded in agreement.

"What did you say?" asked Duchess Diamond Waves. She had just returned from Northern Prance and happened to pass by the shoreline on her way back to the academy. The newfound information on the Time Glass from her sage had given her much to think about and discuss with Celestia after class was finished for the day.

"Your Highness!" The old couple bowed to her. "We were just saying how nice it is to see the student colts and fillies having a good time down there. Such a great idea to let them blow off some steam, Duchess."

"Students? From my magic academy?" She raised a brow and trotted to the edge of the cliff. As she stepped forward in between them and looked down at the beach, her breath was taken away. It was Princess Celestia! The royal was not teaching a class at all, but instead was building a sand castle with several students, including Rainy Air and Flora. They were all smiling. *Smiling in the face of a crisis*, thought Diamond Waves as she watched Celestia use her magic to place a tiny Monacolt flag in the top of the castle.

Diamond Waves felt so betrayed, she could hardly watch the scene. Celestia was doing the exact opposite of what she had asked her to do! How were the students ever going to be ready unless they spent every chance they had preparing for the worst? The duchess closed her eyes, turned on her hoof, and took off in a canter toward the school. She had to go check the Time Glass and think about a new plan of action.

Down on the beach, little Ambrosia Breeze hid behind the jagged rocks, waiting and staring out at the cerulean-blue horizon line. Gulls flew above, squawking. Her magenta tail was wet and sandy from the tide pool she was crouching over. As soon as she saw the familiar yellow hooves approaching on the sand beside her, Ambrosia popped out from her spot. She shot a zap of orange magic from her horn at the colt. Suddenly, water from the shore began to rise up, spinning itself into a tornado shape. It shot toward Lemon Square at full speed. The colt screamed as the water enveloped him.

Everypony galloped over in a panic. Celestia spread her wings and flew over. When she landed, Lemon Square was looking straight out at Ambrosia from a protective water bubble in awe. "You did it! You did a Water Bubble enchantment!"

"I did!" Ambrosia shouted in elation.

Sandy Shore's jaw was agape. "That's an advanced protection spell!"

"Yes, it is. Well done, Ambrosia." Princess Celestia looked out at their faces, filled with wonder and excitement. She felt the same way. "It sure looks as if you Monacolt ponies are a force to be reckoned with. Now, who else wants to try a Water Bubble enchantment?"

CHAPTER

8

The good News

Now that Diamond Waves was back from Northern Prance, Celestia couldn't wait to share her teaching breakthroughs and delight her friend with the news that her simple lesson plan had worked. Celestia knew that the duchess was going to be so relieved. This whole experience had been so wonderful for Celestia, as well as the students. The daily activities of the last two weeks had filled Princess Celestia with a certain sense of happiness and purpose. If the rising of the sun brought her joy, then the light of young ponies learning under her guidance brought her pure elation. It was the whole reason she made her own Unicorn school back home in Canterlot a constant priority.

As Celestia walked toward her friend's headmistress office, her hooves even felt lighter, as if they weren't even adorned with heavily embellished gold hoofcuffs. The students here in Monacolt were bright and eager, not undisciplined and petulant like she'd expected. They just needed to be shown a different way. Everypony in Monacolt was going to be all right, no matter what mysterious foes came to attack them.

If there *were* any foes at all, that was. Celestia was growing increasingly suspicious of the magic behind the Time Glass. Ever since Diamond Waves had left, the sand in the glass had appeared to be falling down the funnel, yet the amount of sand in the top basin seemed unchanged. Princess Celestia was hoping to point out this oddity to the duchess today. Something was off.

The Alicorn trotted past a succession of tall, open windows. The frames were arched at the top just like the ones back in Canterlot Castle. Celestia thought of home and wondered what might be occurring at this very moment. Since it was almost time to lower the sun, Celestia imagined that Luna was probably resting up. In her absence, Princess Luna was tasked with ushering the sun down as well as welcoming the moon once it was time to do so. It took a lot of energy. Princess Twilight was probably going over the graduation-day speech again, practicing the way to say each part in front of a mirror. Princess Celestia chuckled at the idea. She couldn't wait to see them all at the graduation ceremony and Summer Sun Celebration when she got home.

"Something funny, Celestia?" Duchess Diamond Waves appeared in the south doorway. She frowned in concern and looked down at the stone floor. "Perhaps the hopelessness of my situation?"

"Not at all. Actually, it's just the opposite, Diamond!" Celestia exclaimed with a smile. She trotted over and embraced her friend. "I have been waiting to tell you the wonderful news—your students are incredibly bright. So talented! A few of them even managed to perform Fire of Friendship spells *and* Water Bubble enchantments. Those two spells alone can guarantee your safety from attack, I assure you—"

"But that's impossible!" Duchess Diamond Waves exclaimed, her mouth agape. "We've tried and...What I mean to say is—these students have proven...that they have no talent next to taking up space." Diamond's eyes flashed something dark. *And playing around during school hours*, she thought.

"Surely, you're teasing." Celestia was taken aback. "Right, Di?"

"Of course!" Diamond Waves shook the thought away and forced a smile. "I'm so pleased you've made a breakthrough." She didn't seem pleased. Her body was stiff and her movements robotic. The stress of the situation was clearly getting to Diamond Waves. Why else would she say such a mean thing when her students had shown such progress?

"Why don't we go for a walk to the sea and I can tell you all about it?" Celestia motioned her hoof toward the window. In the distance peeking through the buildings, she could see the ocean, blue and serene. "I find it can be rather restorative. Even without the gentle sound of the waves."

"Oh, so you noticed that." Duchess Diamond Waves shifted uncomfortably, her eyes darting to the window. "Fine," she finally answered, leading the way. "Just don't try to make me build a sand castle."

CHAPTER

9

Making Waves

It didn't take long for the two ponies to find Unicorn Cove, the gorgeous little beach outside of the city limits. Princess Celestia could feel herself relaxing a bit as she got farther from the city. She walked out toward the shore. With each step, her hooves sank into the damp sand. It was so quiet here. Almost silent. She looked out to the ocean and imagined the crashing sound of waves. The water was completely still.

Diamond Waves was looking out to the water with a wistful expression. She turned to Celestia. "So, tell me about the students."

"Yes," Celestia brightened. "There is something that you can do, and I guarantee they will pass the exam. It's been working thus far."

"What is it?" Diamond asked, her voice flat. "Cast some sort of concentration spell over them?"

"Heavens, no!" Celestia smirked. "Better concentration is the last thing they need. What they should have is..." She took a few steps forward toward the water's edge and, without warning, dove straight into the sea. The Alicorn jumped and splashed around, kicking up water onto the duchess, whose expression was less than amused. Celestia laughed at her friend's sour face and splashed her again. Drops of water sparkled in the sunlight as they landed on Diamond.

"Celestia!" Diamond Waves shouted through pieces of wet blue mane that were stuck to her forehead. "What do you think you're doing?!"

"Just having a bit of fun!" Celestia sing-songed. "You should try it."

Diamond Waves looked shocked for a moment, insulted by the implication that her old friend thought she didn't know how to have a good time. Diamond had practically invented the concept when she was a young pony. So the blue Unicorn dove into the sea herself, creating a huge splash that drenched Princess Celestia in return. Soon, the two ponies each started to laugh at how silly the other looked. They pulled themselves from the water and sat down the dry sand, trying to catch their breath between giggles. It was just like old times.

Diamond Waves exhaled deeply and looked up to the orange-colored sky. The sun was setting. Celestia smiled as she watched its descent, thinking of the rising moon and her sister. After a few silent, pensive moments, the gentle sound of waves crashing onto the shore began. It was hushed. *Whoosh, swish. Whoosh, swish.*

The duchess bolted upright, her horn glowing with a soft blue magic light. The color grew brighter as she stood up on her hooves and faced the ocean. Soon, the waves were larger—big enough for a pony to surf on! Diamond Waves smiled genuinely and turned to Celestia. "Finally! What a gorgeous sight to behold!"

"Your ability to create waves on the shores of Monacolt has returned," Celestia observed with a knowing smirk. Diamond didn't have to tell Celestia that her talent had gone missing. Everypony knew.

"I can't believe it...." Diamond Waves shed a tear of joy. She wiped it away with her hoof. "I thought I'd lost my magical abilities. On top of the students not passing their exams and the impending doom of my kingdom, I was having an awful time."

"But now you're not. Everything is not always as it seems," assured Celestia. "The ocean is deep. Just because there are no waves on the surface does not mean that things aren't happening beneath. And that's exactly what I was hoping to show you." Princess Celestia stood tall, mane and tail glittering as her wet locks flowed into the wind. "Your magic is still within you."

"I don't understand...." Diamond Waves shook her head. "What did you do?"

"What were you doing the moment your magic returned to you?" Celestia queried, raising a brow. "What were *we* doing?"

"Splashing in the water and—"

"*Laughing,*" Princess Celestia said. "You were having a great time, were you not?"

"Well, yes..." Duchess Diamond Waves wrinkled her nose. "What does that have to do with *my* magic? With anypony's magic?"

"It has everything to do with it, dear friend." Celestia smiled. She began to trot along the shore, and Diamond Waves took up next to her. "The problem that you've been having with yourself—with your talent of making waves in the ocean—is the exact same reason your students cannot complete their spells! You're being too hard on them. They need to relax. It's the only way to achieve great and powerful magic. It's something I have proven in recent moons through my mentoring of Twilight Sparkle. She showed great promise as a student, but she only achieved her true magical potential when she learned to make friends and embrace communal amusement."

"It can't be as simple as that," Diamond Waves said with a shiver.

"Why not?" Celestia stood up and closed her eyes. Pink magic glittered from her horn and enveloped the two ponies in a warm whirlwind of air until they were both completely dry. "You're making things too hard on yourself."

"You're wrong," Duchess Diamond Waves said, turning back to the ocean. Her jaw clenched. "The only reason I haven't been able to create waves is because the attack on Monacolt is growing nearer. According to the Time Glass, everything is off. It's not *me*." As she spoke, the crashing waves of the sea grew smaller and smaller until they were back to the way they'd been before. The only noise was the sound of the seabirds above, cawing at one another and flapping their wings.

Diamond looked to Celestia with an irritated expression. "I asked you here to help prepare my students by *teaching* them, not playing around with them and having fun. I saw you with them today on the beach. That was supposed to be class time. If you don't think you can respect that, Celie, well…"

"Well…what?" Celestia replied, using her most gentle tone.

Diamond sighed. "Well, then I think you should go back to Canterlot. I'll take care of my students and my citizens from here." The duchess turned on her hoof and galloped back toward the city, her words hanging heavy in the stillness of the silent ocean air.

"There she is!" a voice called out from above. "Your Highness!" It was Glimmering Shield, one of Celestia's Royal Guard attendants. He soared down to the beach from the high cliff, wings outstretched. Golden Flight followed right behind him. As the two ponies' hooves met the sand, they exchanged a worried look.

"My kinsponies," Princess Celestia said with a bow. "Is there a problem?"

Glimmering Shield bowed back to her. "We've received a letter from Princesses Luna and Twilight Sparkle. There are also reports from the head of the Royal Guard and the mayor of Horseshoe Bay." Golden Flight passed her the scrolls. "It's the Carcinus, Princess. I'm afraid...there's been another attack on Canterlot."

CHAPTER

10

A Letter from Home

Dear Princess Celestia,

By now, you've likely had word
from the Royal Guard about
the Carcinus entering Canterlot's
borders, but I assure you that
there is no cause for alarm! Some
of the citizens panicked when
they saw a twenty-foot-tall crab

walking toward the castle, that's all. Princess Luna and I have the situation completely under control. She knows the Carcinus and is currently escorting him back to Horseshoe Bay.

I have studied these creatures extensively in many books, but I had to go to the library and refresh my knowledge on the subject. It is generally understood that despite their intimidating appearance Carcinus are quite gentle creatures; however, they do tend to get surly when ignored, which is exactly

what happened in this case. The
Carcinus was upset over some
ponies that built new cottages right
next to his cave on the beach and
he tried to befriend them. Since
Carcinus don't speak pony, they
thought he was attacking. Princess
Luna is going to set it all straight
and I am going to stay here and
watch over Canterlot.

Since the Unicorn academy
students had finished their exams
for the moon and were just
awaiting their results, I treated
some of them to a reading from

<u>Star Swirl's Seven Principles of</u>
<u>Unicorn Magic: Third Edition</u>,
including some of the hoofnotes!
I think they really enjoyed it! I
also assigned them a solid summer
reading list. You still do those,
right? That was always my
favorite part of school.

Hope everything is going well out
there in Monacolt!

Sincerely,

(Still) Your Faithful Student-
Princess Twilight Sparkle

Princess Celestia used her magic to close the scroll, placing it on the desk next to the reports from the Royal Guard and the mayor of Horseshoe Bay. Each of the messages had been different in tone—the mayor's report was panicky and the Royal Guard's report was rife with subtle requests for Celestia to return to Canterlot. But the one from her fellow princess was calm. She'd read Twilight Sparkle's letter three times and still couldn't find anything in it to show that Equestria was truly in danger.

If Luna was going to solve the Carcinus issue, then Equestria was in good hooves. Her younger sister had always had a special talent for talking with animals. Back when the two of them had first become princesses, Luna had even befriended a manticore named Melvin, as well as helped to solve the griffon disagreement. Celestia theorized that it was Luna's ability to speak to ponies through dreams that had helped her to learn how to communicate in unconventional methods. She just saw things in a new way, a different light.

Princess Celestia gazed out the window of her lush guest quarters at the Monacolt Magic Academy. The moon hung high in the sky, bright as ever. *Everything is fine, right, Luna?* she wondered. *Or shall I go back to Equestria?* A soft knock came at the door, interrupting Celestia's troubled thoughts.

When she opened it, nopony was there. But on the floor there was a shiny red apple. Celestia used her magic to pick it up and saw that there was a tiny note attached. In messy hoofwriting, it said:

Dear Princess Celestia,

Look! I did the apple spell you showed me on your first day! You are the best teacher ever.

Love, Rainy Air

Princess Celestia caught her reflection staring back at her on the surface of the apple. She hadn't even realized she was smiling so wide. That settled it. There were still lessons being learned here in Monacolt, and she was going to be the one to teach them. Canterlot could wait just a little longer.

CHAPTER

11

Nighttime Glass

The sounds of laughter and magic echoed from the dormitories and down the hallways of the Monacolt Magic Academy. Celestia wandered through the building, searching for Diamond Waves, but she was nowhere to be found. She'd looked for her friend all day, hoping to apologize for their little argument the previous night. But Celestia knew that her friend was quite stubborn and probably avoiding her. She hated to lose, to be proven wrong.

It was just like a certain instance long ago when Celestia was visiting Monacolt for a summit with the Maretonians. The duchess had invited everypony down to the beach to play a traditional game. The goal was for each player to build a castle out of sand without using the aid of their magic, and the pony with the tallest castle won. Diamond Waves had boasted about her skills all evening, and sure enough, she impressed everypony with a beautiful sand tower complete with delicate turrets and a moat around the bottom. However, when the Duke of Maretonia sneezed, the thing came crashing down into a heap of glittering sand. Everypony laughed and after that, Diamond refused to ever play the game again.

The more Celestia thought about their current situation, the more she was surprised that Diamond Waves had ever even asked her to come help in the first place. But it didn't matter. Princess Celestia wasn't leaving Monacolt until she finished what she'd started. It was the only way to save the land and her friendship.

Later that night, Celestia dreamt of falling through a giant hourglass of golden sand. She landed softly on the bottom, but realized she was caught behind the glass, watching as Diamond Waves wandered around outside of it, calling out her name. When Princess Celestia tried to use her magic, the glass spun around. Suddenly, it stopped, and then Princess Luna was inside the glass, too! Next to her stood a gigantic red crab with huge claws. He waved at her. "Greetings, sister," Luna said with a chuckle. "This is Carcinus. Sorry to come to you in a dream like this, I know how you hate it when I do that. I just thought it was easier than writing a letter."

"It's a welcome visit," Princess Celestia replied as she embraced her sister. "Is everything all right?"

"I'm the one who should be asking you that question." Luna raised her eyebrow and looking around at their hourglass-shaped cage. "Are you okay, sister?"

"Yes, of course I am." Princess Celestia

frowned. "I'm clearly only dreaming of the Time Glass because it is what plagues Duchess Diamond Waves. She believes that as soon as the sand runs out, a great attack will take place on her ponies and Monacolt."

"This wouldn't be the same Time Glass that King Nautilus had, would it?" Luna asked. She placed her hoof on the glass wall and looked to the engravings on the outside. "The one that was a gift from the griffon king Grover?"

"It very well could be," Princess Celestia replied. Outside, she could still see the dream version of Diamond Waves in distress. "What do you know about this artifact?"

Luna smiled knowingly. "The sands of time will never run their course on it. It flows forever."

"What would be the purpose of that, little sister?"

"It was a training tool designed to keep their Griffon Royal Guard ready to protect the kingdom at any time," Luna continued. "It's clever. The griffons realized that a guard at the ready was kept on his claws more than one who believed his kingdom to be safe. Thus, the illusion of an imminent attack."

Celestia nodded, adding up the parts. "Diamond Waves must have misinterpreted the meaning of her father's gift of the Time Glass and read it as her duty and destiny."

"Does this mean your work here in Monacolt is finished?" Luna asked. Her face was hopeful, yet tired. "Now that you know the ponies will be safe?"

"No," Princess Celestia looked back and forth from the Carcinus to Luna. "There's only one way to show Diamond Waves that everypony here is truly safe. And that is to stage a fake attack." Celestia trotted over the giant crab. "Once the duchess sees that her students can handle a dangerous situation on their own, it will prove to her that they are ready for her to let them go."

"It sounds like it could work," Luna agreed with a nod. Her blue mane sparkled beautifully against the swirling sand. "What do you have in mind?"

Celestia gestured to the Carcinus. "I don't suppose you know any gigantic creatures that owe you a favor, do you?" The two sisters shared a smile, and then Princess Celestia woke up.

CHAPTER

12

Failed Exams

The next morning, Princess Celestia entered the classroom to begin her lessons for the day, but there was nopony there. Her mind felt hazy, and she wondered for a moment if she was still dreaming. She touched her hoof to her face and felt the coolness of her hoofcuff against her cheek.

It was definitely morning, and this was all happening for real. Perhaps the students were running late. She took a seat at the desk in the front of the room to wait for them and gather her thoughts.

Princess Luna had visited her last night. Princess Celestia didn't usually like when Luna appeared in her dreams, as it felt invasive for somepony so close to her to be able to explore her subconscious mind. But the dream she'd had this time was productive. She had always suspected that there was something off about the Time Glass, and now she understood why. Soon, Duchess Diamond Waves would as well.

"Try it again!" Princess Celestia heard a faint voice say. She stood up and followed the sound, which grew louder as she approached the Mane Hall. "Everypony, let's focus a little more, okay?"

It was the voice of Duchess Diamond Waves. Her blue mane and yellow hide shone bright across the dark hall. She was pacing back in forth in front of the students, who were all lined up in a perfect row against the wall facing her. In the middle of the room was a large tub of water. Ambrosia Breeze stood next to it, looking down at the ground. She seemed dejected.

"Come on, Ambrosia Breeze," Diamond Waves encouraged. "Everypony says they saw you do it. I just really want to see, too!" The duchess held up a clipboard and a quill and stared down the young filly. "As soon as you show me the Water Bubble enchantment, you'll be done." Ambrosia shifted back and forth from hoof to hoof. She looked to her classmates and bit her magenta-colored lip. "I...can't."

"Look, students. I didn't want to scare you, but I think you should know that—"

"I'm leaving soon," Princess Celestia interrupted, trotting into the room. "And I shall have to say good-bye."

"You will?" Rainy Air whimpered.

"Princess Celestia, please don't go!" cried Sandy Shore.

"But what about the party on the beach we were planning?" Flora squeaked, flipping her teal mane away from her sad, sweet lavender face. "I already made hats."

The tension was palpable, but Princess Celestia looked up to her friend's face. "What do you say, Di?"

Diamond Waves looked like she couldn't hold on to her stress any longer. She threw her hooves up in surrender. "Fine, students. Go and have your party on the beach with Princess Celestia." Diamond Waves used her magic to clean up the basin of water. "We weren't making progress, anyway. It's no use."

"Wow! Thank you, Headmistress!" The students lit up. "So cool!" They cantered back to their rooms to get their beach items. All except for Flora, who was only retrieving her elaborate hoof-made party hats.

"Sure," Diamond Waves replied, cracking a fake smile. "Uh, have fun." She took a look around the empty room. It looked even bigger with all the furniture pushed to the sides like it had been for the test. The duchess sighed, her face showing signs of defeat. She'd lost hope.

"Are you coming?" Princess Celestia asked. She used her magic to set all the tables and chairs straight with one jolt. "Down to the beach?"

"No." Diamond Waves shook her head, overcome with emotion. "I have to go to my quarters and reread the prophecy. Maybe there's a clue I'm missing that could predict when exactly the attack is going to happen. Then I'll know how to prepare."

Celestia trotted over to her friend and hugged her. "Relax and come with me. This will be over soon."

"How do you know that?" Diamond Waves asked.

"Have you seen the Time Glass today?" Celestia raised her brows in mock terror.

"The sands have near run out, Diamond. It is time to meet your destiny. Hurry up, it's waiting."

CHAPTER

13

Attack on Monacolt

The two tall ponies tore through the streets of Monacolt, past the dockyards, and toward the wooden steps to the beachfront. Celestia led the way, clearing the busy tourist hoof traffic. When they reached the cliffside, Princess Celestia finally took off, spreading her vast white wings. She soared through the air alongside the seagulls and landed on the soft sand right into the middle of the party. The duchess arrived a moment later, slightly frazzled and out of breath. She looked around the beach, expectant. The students were practically the only ponies in sight.

"What took you ponies so long?" Ambrosia Breeze, who was wearing a crown that looked just like Celestia's, giggled. It was gold with three points and a large purple jewel in the center. "We've been waiting to start the castle game."

"The castle game?" Duchess Diamond Waves asked.

"We build sand castles," Rainy Air explained. He was wearing a black top hat. "No magic allowed, just hoofpower. The pony with the highest tower wins!"

"I know this game...." Diamond shook

her head as she met eyes with Celestia. "Princess Celestia and I used to play it when we were younger."

"You did?" marveled Lemon Square as he straightened his Star Swirl the Bearded–style wizard hat. "Who won?"

"That's not important," Princess Celestia insisted. Her mane and tail flowed into a nearby in-progress sand castle. "What's important is that we had fun—"

"Celestia *always* won," Diamond Waves interrupted, turning toward the students and the back of the cliff, her body framed by the blue ocean. Her voice suddenly grew serious. "In fact, Celestia has always known better about everything. And why shouldn't she—she's a thousand moons old!" The duchess began to smile as the realization hit her. "Celie, what if you were right about me not having to worry? There might be no attack at all!"

"Attack?" Sandy Shore asked, scratching his short white mane. "Like the Muybridge?"

"Like that gigantic crab emerging from the ocean right now?" Flora squeaked. She pointed her hoof to the water. Everypony stared at her blankly. *SNAP! SNAP!* The sound of two giant claws sounded out across the beach. The ponies spun around and were met with the sight of a massive red crab that was more than twenty feet tall!

"A Carcinus!" Duchess Diamond Waves shrieked in a mixture of horror and delight at being right all along. She looked to Princess Celestia for guidance, but the royal had disappeared. So Diamond Waves did what any good teacher would do. She stood tall in front of her students, shielding them from the terrifying beast that was advancing toward them at an alarming rate of speed. Then she focused her magic and closed her eyes.

Suddenly, the waves began to crash.

With each splash upon the shore, the crab slowed down, getting swept up in the surf. But it wasn't enough to stop him. Ambrosia Breeze looked to her friends, her fellow students. She met eyes with Sandy Shore and Rainy Air. Flora followed close behind with Lemon Square. The others were not far behind.

The young ponies formed a semicircle around the Carcinus, remaining calm. Then something incredible happened. Diamond Waves opened her eyes just in time to see her students performing the most perfect group Water Bubble enchantment she'd ever seen in her life. They shot their horns at the water, creating several small tornadoes. As their magic joined, the tornadoes grew and grew until finally it was one large cylinder of sea. The water surged forward, surrounding the vicious-looking crab and encasing him in a spherical water cage. He was unharmed but contained.

Duchess Diamond Waves was shocked at how quickly the attack had been controlled. There had been a real, monstrous threat to the city, just as she'd always feared. But now Monacolt was safe, and it was all thanks to her fearless young students. Princess Celestia had taught them everything they needed to know after all. Suddenly, Diamond was searching to remember why she'd ever doubted her in the first place.

CHAPTER 14

Wave good-bye

As Princess Celestia stepped into her carriage, she felt a sense of pride. The faces of the young Magic Academy graduates stared back at her in admiration and sadness at her departure from their fair city. The ponies waved at her, shouting well wishes for her journey back to Canterlot and hopes for her to return to visit soon. Princess Celestia had accomplished what she'd sought out to do in Monacolt by helping her friends see some new ways of looking at learning and had learned a few lessons of her own.

As Duchess Diamond Waves trotted up to the carriage, her mane and tail were moving and glittering even though there was no breeze in the air. The golden band across her forehead glistened in the sunlight as she smiled and hugged Celestia. She looked like her old self again. "Thank you for everything, Princess." She leaned forward and whispered into Celestia's ear. "Especially that letter where you explained everything. It makes the victory a little less sweet, but it makes a whole lot more sense!"

Princess Celestia laughed. "I hope you're

not too upset with me for setting everything up with Luna."

"Not at all," Diamond Waves admitted. "It was perfect."

"Actually, I was thinking we could make this a yearly thing? Maybe use it as the test on the new class of ponies? It sounds like a lot of *fun*...." Princess Celestia said, raising an eyebrow. "Doesn't it, Diamond Waves?"

"I don't know about that...." The duchess made a serious face and put her hoof up to her chin. Finally, she laughed. "Only joking. It sounds like a total blast!" Princess Celestia could hear the laughter of the young graduates as she took off into the pink-and-orange sky toward the prettiest sunset she'd ever seen.

Dear reader,

I made these bonus pages just for you! Have fun filling them out and sharing them with your friends.

Yours,
Princess Celestia

Like Day and Night

As reigning princesses, Celestia and Luna are responsible for raising the sun and the moon each day and night. The ponies of Equestria appreciate it very much. They love to play in the beautiful sunshine and admire the gorgeous moon as they drift off to sleep. What are some of your favorite things about each time of day? List them below!

DAY	NIGHT
Playing outside at the park	Snuggling up in pajamas with a bedtime story
Blue skies	Twinkling stars

Foal-proof Test Advice

The ponies at the Monacolt Magic Academy are
nervous about passing their big final exam.
Have you ever taken a test or worked on a project
at school that made you feel anxious? What did
you do to calm your nerves? If you had to give
advice to a friend, what would you say?
Use the lines below to write about it.

_____

_____

_____

_____

_____

_____

_____

_____

_____

Making Waves

What is a beach without the sound of the tide? Princess Celestia's friend from Monacolt, Duchess Diamond Waves, has a magic talent for making waves in the ocean, but she's lost it. Can you help her find her special skill again by drawing your own waves next to the beach? Make the waves as big or as little as you like!

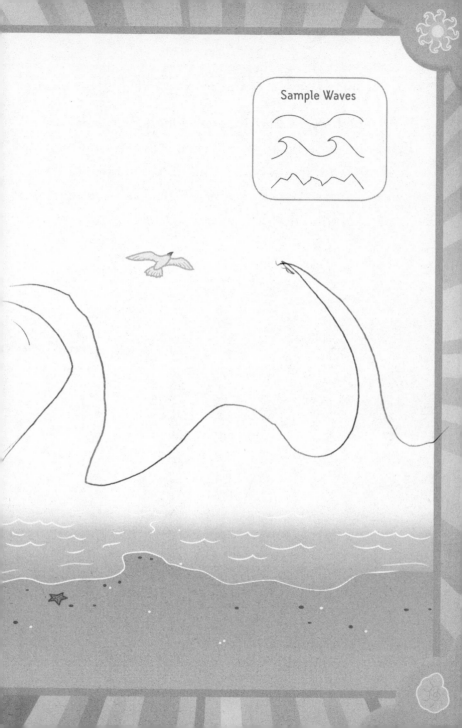

Sample Waves

Mind Your Banners

The halls of the Monacolt Magic Academy are decorated with beautiful banners representing the royals of the land. If you had a kingdom, what would be on your banner? Use the blank ones below to design your royal emblem! Hint: Draw your favorite cutie mark.

Dear Faithful Student

Throughout the years, Princess Celestia has taught many ponies about magic, but there hasn't been a single pony who's learned more about the Magic of Friendship han Princess Twilight Sparkle! Princess Twilight has written Celestia lots of letters about the lessons she's learned with her friends in Ponyville. Use the template below to write a letter back to Twilight from Celestia herself.

Dear Faithful Student,

Thank you for your wonderful letter about your friend

_____! _____
    (friend's name)   *(friendship lesson)*

is such a great lesson to learn. I hope you will share this

valuable information with _____ and
                                 (friend's name)

_____. I hope all is well in Ponyville.
   (friend's name)

I look forward to visiting you during _____
                                   (holiday)

next month!

Regards,

Princess Celestia

Castles in the Sand

Princess Celestia is teaching the students in Monacolt a new game. The goal is to build the tallest sand castle on the beach without using magic. If you were playing, what kind of castle would you build? Use the space below to draw your sand castle. Be creative and don't forget to give it a cool name!

My castle is called
Sprinkles.

Snack Attack

When Celestia meets the young pony Rainy Air for the first time, he's been studying so hard that he's grown hungry. The young pony is out looking for a snack. When the princess does a fancy spell to procure a fresh apple for him, he's amazed and excited for the yummy treat. If you could do a magic spell to make snacks appear, what would you choose?

At a party _____

In the summer _____

At school _____

In the winter _____

At home _____

Anytime! _____

Shell Scramble

The ponies of the Monacolt Magic Academy
are finally on summer break! To celebrate, Ambrosia
Breeze has invited some of the other students to
the beach to collect shells. Things are going great
until Lemon Square accidentally knocks over
the buckets and mixes up the shells! Can you help
the ponies match the shells on the left with
their partners on the right?

Fire of Friendship

Nothing can warm a pony's heart like friendship, except maybe Celestia's fiery sun! Use the heart below to fill in some words to describe one of your best friends. Hint: *Silly*, *fun*, and *kind* are all great words.

Finding the Right Words

Sometimes it can be hard to speak up in class!
The ponies at the Monacolt Magic Academy can't
seem to find the right words today. Can you help
them by circling the words below?

CELESTIA

DUCHESS

FRIENDSHIP

LESSON

MAGIC

OCEAN

PRINCESS

STUDENT

WAVE

```
F N O S S E L W M L
A R P P C T B K J Z
D I I R O I Z K T D
U P T E I C G N V J
C M V S N N E A N M
H W A V E D C A M M
E Q J D U L S E N T
S G N T T R E H S G
S W S Z V P D C I S
P B R Q B B V Y W P
```

Pretty Postcards

Princess Celestia and Duchess Diamond Waves
are friends who don't see each other very often
because they live far away. Do you have any friends or
relatives who live far away from you? Use the space
below to draw them a postcard of your city.
Don't forget to write them a note on the back!

GREETINGS FROM

Celestia's Friendship Letters

As the wise and majestic leader of Equestria,
Princess Celestia has many admirable qualities that
make all ponies respect and love her. She's a teacher,
a friend, and lots of other wonderful things.
Use the letters of Celestia's name to find nice words
to describe her. Twilight Sparkle has already filled
in two to help you. When you're finished, give
your own name the royal treatment!

C *Clever*

E _____

L *Loyal*

E _____

S _____

T _____

I _____

A _____

Sun and Moon

Princess Celestia and Princess Luna are quite different, even though they are sisters. Some ponies say they are opposites. Can you name the opposite of each of the words below? Write the answers on the lines provided.

WORD	OPPOSITE
hot	_cold_
up	_____
light	_____
happy	_____
long	_____